P9-CTQ-161

E MCALLISTER
McAllister, Angela.
Trust me, Mom! /

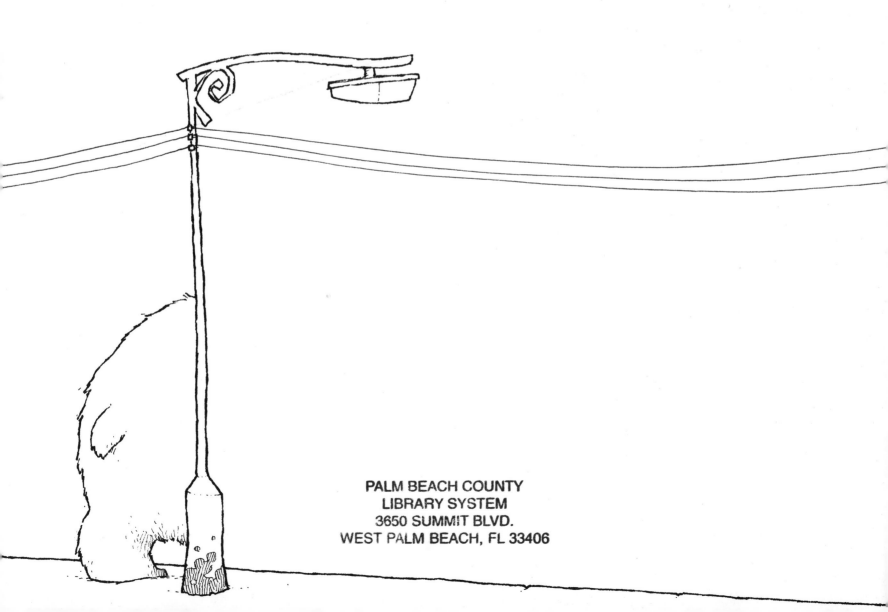

**PALM BEACH COUNTY
LIBRARY SYSTEM
3650 SUMMIT BLVD.
WEST PALM BEACH, FL 33406**

Trust Me, Mom!

For Simon – A.M.
For Derek – R.C.

BLOOMSBURY
CHILDREN'S
BOOKS

Text copyright © 2005 by Angela McAllister
Illustrations copyright © 2005 by Ross Collins

All rights reserved. No part of this book may be used or reproduced in any manner whatsoever without written
permission from the publisher, except in the case of brief quotations embodied in critical articles or reviews.

Typeset in Old Claude
The art was created with watercolors and acrylics

Published by Bloomsbury Publishing, New York, London, and Berlin.
Distributed to the trade by Holtzbrinck Publishers

Library of Congress Cataloging-in-Publication Data
McAllister, Angela.
Trust me, Mom! / by Angela McAllister ; illustrated by Ross Collins.–1st U.S. ed.
p. cm.
Summary: Ollie tries to be safe and polite on his first walk to the corner store alone, even when scary creatures appear on the way.
ISBN-10: 1-58234-955-X (hc)
ISBN-13: 978-1-58234-955-8 (hc)
[1. Growth–Fiction. 2. Mother and child–Fiction. 3. Humorous stories.] I. Collins, Ross, ill.
PZ7.M11714Tr 2005   [E]–dc22   2004060883

First U.S. Edition 2005
Printed in China by South China Printing Co.
3 5 7 9 10 8 6 4 2

Bloomsbury Publishing, Children's Books, U.S.A.
175 Fifth Avenue, New York, NY 10010

All papers used by Bloomsbury Publishing are natural, recyclable products made from wood grown in well-managed forests.
The manufacturing processes conform to the environmental regulations of the country of origin.

Trust Me, Mom!

by **Angela McAllister**

illustrated by **Ross Collins**

BLOOMSBURY
CHILDREN'S
BOOKS

Today
was the day.

For the first time, Ollie
was allowed to cross the road
and walk to the store by himself.

Mom had practiced with him.

"Now," she said. "Go straight there and don't stop to talk to anyone.

Don't put your hands in your pockets, in case you trip.

Look and listen before
you cross the road."

"And I won't walk on the cracks in the sidewalk,"
said Ollie, "or the bears will get me."

"No," said Mom.

"That's only in stories."

"Don't take the shortcut through Mr. Spinelli's yard. Don't stop to read comics in the store. Just ask for cheese."

"Can I buy candy too?" said Ollie.

"PLEASE is the magic word, Oliver," said Mom.

"PLEASE can I buy candy too?"

"Yes, but don't get Fireball Fizzers. They're so strong, they'll blow your head off. And remember to check the change."

"Trust me, Mom," said Ollie. "I can look after myself."

And off he went.

Ollie walked along the road, humming happily.
But as soon as he turned the corner, a
bug-eyed monster jumped out at him.

Mom hadn't warned him about monsters.

"Ggrraaaagh!!"
roared the monster wildly.

"GGGRRRAAAGGGHH!!!"

roared Ollie, even wilder.

The bug-eyed monster hadn't been warned about boys. With a yelp he turned tail and ran away.

Ollie continued down the road. He passed a spooky house.
Out of the window floated a ghost.

Mom hadn't warned him about ghosts.

"Whooooh!"

the ghost moaned at him.

"Sorry," said Ollie. "I believe in Santa Claus and the Tooth Fairy, but I've NEVER believed in ghosts."

For a moment the ghost looked disappointed, then it faded away like a sad puff of breath.

Ollie came to the crosswalk. He looked and listened.
He crossed safely. Now which way, he wondered.
The long path by the library or the
shortcut through Mr. Spinelli's yard?

Ollie sighed and
took the long path.

Around the corner of the library came a witch on a bicycle.
She bumped into Ollie and dropped her books.

WITCH GUIDE

21 NASTY THINGS
To Do To KITTENS

BROOM FLIGHT
for BEGINNERS

Turning Monkeys
into Donkeys

Mom hadn't warned him about witches.

"Aargh!"

screeched the witch. "Pick up my books
or I'll turn you into a pile of skunk poo."

"No, I won't," said Ollie. "Go away."

The witch cackled. "Only MAGIC words make witches go away!"

"Abracadabra!" "Hocus Pocus!"
said Ollie.

Nothing happened.   The witch grinned.

Then Ollie remembered.

"PLEASE go away!"

At these words, the
witch screamed
and disappeared

in a puff
of smoke.

Ollie arrived at the store. He asked for the cheese and chose some candy. He also wanted Fireball Fizzers.

"I'll just take two," he said. "Small ones."

Ollie checked his change,
peeked at the comics,
and then he set off for home.

I'm doing fine, thought Ollie.

He scrambled through
Mr. Spinelli's yard and crossed
the road safely. Suddenly
a grizzly bear appeared.

Mom hadn't warned him about bears.

"**Rrrrraagh!**" growled the grizzly.

It looked hungry. Ollie decided to run.

He ran down the sidewalk, stepping on every crack he could. Sure enough, three huge bears stepped out from behind a lamppost. They saw the grizzly. It saw them.

Ollie skipped out of the way just as the bear fight began.

"Can't stop!"
called Ollie.

Ollie turned the corner. He was nearly home. Suddenly there was a flash of light, and two aliens stood before him.

Mom hadn't warned him about aliens.

"Take us to your leader," they said in thin, squeaky voices.

"That could be difficult," said Ollie. "I'd be late getting home."

He took a piece of candy out of his bag and popped it in his mouth.

Then he offered the aliens his Fireball Fizzers.

The aliens inspected the candy,
then popped them into their mouths.

"Yerk!" they shrieked.

At once, steam shot out of their ears,

When Ollie got home, he gave Mom the correct change.

"Did you do as I told you?" she asked.

"I didn't put my hands in my pockets," he said truthfully.

"I knew you'd be all right, Ollie," said Mom.

Ollie went out into the yard to finish his candy.

"I told you to trust me, Mom. I CAN look after myself."

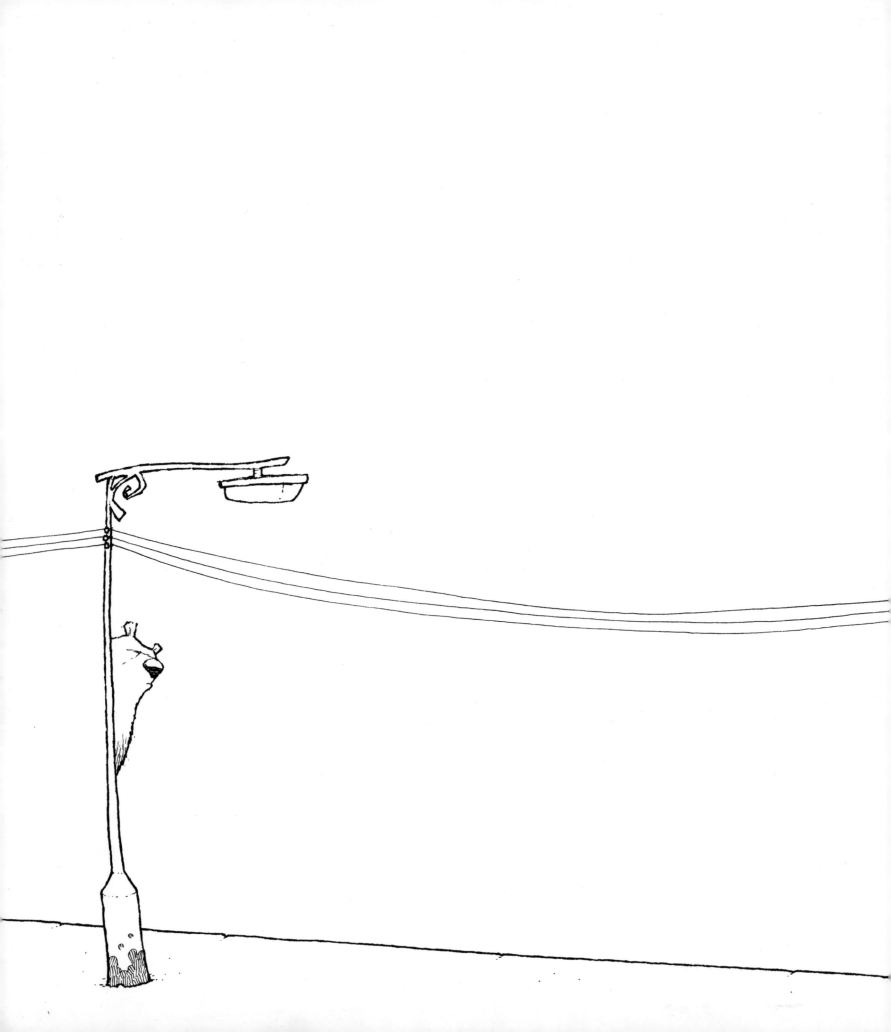